Heidi

Retold from the Johanna Spyri original
by Lisa Church

Illustrated by Jamel Akib

Sterling Publishing Co., Inc.
New York

Library of Congress Cataloging-in-Publication Data

Church, Lisa R., 1960–
 Heidi / retold from the Johanna Spyri original by Lisa Church ; illustrated by Jamel Akib ; afterword by Arthur Pober.
  p. cm.—(Classic starts)
 Summary: An abridged version of Johanna Spyri's classic story of a Swiss orphan who is heartbroken when she must leave her beloved grandfather and their happy home in the mountains to go to school and to care for an invalid girl in the city.
 ISBN-13: 978-1-4027-3691-9
 ISBN-10: 1-4027-3691-6
 [1. Orphans—Fiction. 2. Grandfathers—Fiction. 3. Mountain life—Switzerland—Fiction. 4. Switzerland—History—19th century—Fiction.] I. Akib, Jamel, ill. II. Spyri, Johanna, 1827–1901. Heidi. III. Title. IV. Series.

PZ7.C4703Hei 2007
[Fic]—dc22

                                                                        2006014670
                      2 4 6 8 10 9 7 5 3 1

                 Published by Sterling Publishing Co., Inc.
                387 Park Avenue South, New York, NY 10016
                       Copyright © 2007 by Lisa Church
                    Illustrations copyright © 2007 by Jamel Akib
                   Distributed in Canada by Sterling Publishing
                  ^c/o Canadian Manda Group, 165 Dufferin Street,
                       Toronto, Ontario, Canada M6K 3H6
         Distributed in the United Kingdom by GMC Distribution Services,
         Castle Place, 166 High Street, Lewes, East Sussex, England BN7 1XU
             Distributed in Australia by Capricorn Link (Australia) Pty. Ltd.
                    P.O. Box 704, Windsor, NSW 2756, Australia

           Classic Starts is a trademark of Sterling Publishing Co., Inc.

                   Sterling ISBN-13: 978-1-4027-3691-9
                        ISBN-10: 1-4027-3691-6

       For information about custom editions, special sales, premium and
            corporate purchases, please contact Sterling Special Sales
        Department at 800-805-5489 or specialsales@sterlingpub.com.

CONTENTS

∽

CHAPTER 1

Up the Mountain

∽

"Heidi, keep up!"

The words stung the ears of the overdressed five-year-old. She nodded to her aunt and hurried her step. The three dresses she had on—one on top of the other—and the thick wool shawl wound about her made her step slow on such a hot June day.

"Are you tired?" Aunt Dete asked.

"No," answered the child. "I am hot."

"We shall soon get to the top. You must walk bravely on a little longer and take good long steps. We will be there in another hour," the woman said in a cheerful voice.

It seemed like hours since they had left Dorfli and begun their way up the footpath. But in truth, it had only been one hour. Just enough time had passed to take them to a small village built into the side of the mountain. People usually stopped here to rest and visit with friends on their way to the top. But today the young woman and the child did not stop to rest. The trip they were on was too important to interrupt with friendly visits.

"If you're going farther up the mountain, I will walk with you, Dete!" a woman called out.

Dete waved and nodded to the woman. She slowed her steps a little so the older lady could join her.

"I suppose this is the child your sister left?" the woman asked when she saw Heidi.

"Yes," answered Dete. "I am taking her to live with her grandfather."

"You're going to leave that child with him? You must be crazy! How can you do such a thing? The old man won't take her in, anyway. He will throw both of you out the minute you arrive!"

"He can't very well do that," Dete answered. "He is her grandfather. I have taken care of her since her mother died when the poor babe was only one. But now I have some great chances coming my way. I am finally going to have a nice place to live and work. It's about time that her grandfather does his duty."

"So you are just going to leave the child with the old man and move away?" the old woman asked in surprise. "It's hard for me to believe that you could do such a thing."

"What do you mean?" asked Dete. "I have done my duty with Heidi! What do you think I should do with her? I can't take her with me!"

The old woman never gave her an answer. The house she was stopping to visit appeared before them. Dete remembered this hut. A younger woman lived there with her mother and her son, Peter. Almost everyone knew the eleven-year-old boy. Each morning he would go down to the valley to fetch the goats. Then he would drive them up the mountain and take care of them until it was time to go home for the night.

"Good luck to you!" the old woman called as she went inside to see Grandmother.

Dete waved her hand and watched as the lady walked toward the small brown hut. She didn't want to admit that her friend could be right. She took a minute to straighten her hat and then turned around to look for Heidi. She needed to get on with her trip.

CHAPTER 2

Meeting Grandfather

⌒ා

Heidi was enjoying watching the goats and the boy who led them. She struggled to keep up with him as he sprang from one rock to another. The layers of clothing she had on prevented her from getting close enough to speak to him.

All at once Heidi sat herself down on the ground. She began pulling off her shoes and stockings as fast as her little fingers could move. When this was done, she unwound the hot red shawl and threw it off. Then she took off her coat, too. There was still another one underneath

to unfasten. Her aunt had put her Sunday coat on atop her everyday one to save her from carrying it. Quick as lightning, this one went, too. Heidi stood up. She was now wearing only the little slip that she had started out with this morning. She put all her clothes together in a tidy little heap and then went jumping and climbing after Peter and the goats.

Peter had barely noticed the girl. When he suddenly saw her appear in her undergarments, his face broke into a grin. Heidi questioned him on everything from the goats' homes to how many there were. She had lost herself in her talking when she arrived at the spot where Dete stood.

"Heidi, what have you been doing? What a sight you have made of yourself! And where are your two coats and the red shawl? And the new shoes I bought and the new stockings I knitted for you—everything is gone! Not a thing left! What were you thinking, Heidi? Where are all your clothes?"

The child quietly pointed to a spot on the mountainside below and answered, "Down there." Dete followed the direction of her finger. She could just make out something lying on the ground. The pile had a spot of red on top of it, which she knew had to be the shawl.

"You rotten little thing!" exclaimed Dete angrily. "What could have made you do something like that? What made you undress yourself? What do you mean by it?"

"I don't want any clothes," said the child.

"You selfish child! Don't you have any sense at all?" Her aunt was red with anger. "Who is going all that way down to get them? It will take a half hour to walk down there! Peter, you go off and fetch them for me as quickly as you can. Get going! *Now!*"

Peter followed the order, completing the run in a shorter amount of time than Dete thought possible. She gave him a coin for his quickness. Peter's face beamed with delight as he put it into his pocket.

The young boy followed Dete and Heidi on the final part of their climb. After almost an hour, they reached the top of the mountain. Grandfather's hut stood on a cliff where every ray of sun could rest upon it. It also had a full view of the valley below. It was a beautiful place.

An old man was sitting outside the hut, watching the three people come toward him. He waited patiently for them to speak first.

"Good evening, Grandfather," Heidi said. The young girl was not shy with her words.

"What is the meaning of this?" her grandfather asked gruffly. He gave the child an abrupt shake of the hand and looked at her from under his bushy eyebrows.

Heidi stared back at him. She couldn't take her eyes off his face! The grandfather before her had a long beard and thick gray eyebrows that grew together over his nose. They looked just like a bush.

"I wish you good day," said Dete when she and Peter finally reached the old man. "I have brought you Tobias and Adelheid's child. You probably don't recognize her. You haven't seen her since she was a baby."

"What has she got to do with me?" the old man asked. "And you, boy," he continued, "be off with your goats! And take mine with you!"

One look at the old man made Peter obey at once. It was easy to see that Heidi's grandfather wanted him gone.

"The child is here to stay with you," Dete said. "I have done my duty by taking care of her over the last four years. Now it is time for you to do yours."

"That's it?" said the old man. He looked at her with a flash in his eye. "And when the child begins to cry and whine after you leave—as they do when they miss homes and mothers—what am I supposed to do with her then?"

"That's your problem," snarled Dete. "I put up with her as a crying baby when her real mother died. It was hard enough to take care of my mother and myself! Now I have the chance to go out and be on my own. I cannot pass this up. You are her nearest relative. You are in charge. And keep in mind that you will have to answer for it if anything happens to the girl."

Heidi's grandfather did not like the way Dete spoke to him. And Dete knew that leaving such a small child with this old man was a horrible thing to do. She felt shame and embarrassment as he kicked her out of his house.

"Good-bye to you then, and to you, too, Heidi," she called. She quickly turned away and started to run down the mountainside.

As she passed the neighbors standing at doors and open windows, Dete heard their cries: "Where is the child? Where have you left the child?"

Her mouth opened, but she couldn't answer. She had left her alone with an old man whom everybody knew was not very nice. Would their cries ever stop ringing in her ears?

CHAPTER 3

At Home with Grandfather

$\backsim$

As soon as Dete disappeared, the old man went back to his bench. He stared at the ground without making a sound. Heidi, meanwhile, was enjoying looking about her new home. She explored until she found a shed built against the hut. This was where the goats were kept, but it was empty. Heidi continued her search and came to the pine trees behind the hut. She listened to the wind whistle through the branches and then headed back to her grandfather. Heidi placed herself in front of the old man and simply stared at him. The old man looked up slowly.

"What is it that you want?" he asked.

"I want to see inside the house," said Heidi.

"Come on, then!" her grandfather said. He rose and walked toward the hut.

"Bring your bundle of clothes in with you," he told her.

"I don't want them anymore," was her quick answer.

The old man turned to look at her. Seeing her dark eyes sparkling with excitement over what she was going to see next made him think about his answer.

"Why don't you want them anymore?" he finally asked.

"Because I want to run around like the goats with their thin light legs."

"Well, you can do that if you like," said her grandfather, "but bring them in anyway. We'll put them in the cupboard."

Heidi did as she was told. The old man opened the door and Heidi stepped inside after him. She found herself in a good-sized room that covered the whole first floor of the hut. In one corner stood Grandfather's bed. In another was the fireplace with a large kettle hanging above it. On the farther side was a large door in the wall. This was the cupboard. Grandfather opened it. Inside were his clothes, cups, glasses, plates, smoked meat, and cheese. Heidi ran to the shelf and thrust in her bundle of clothing as quickly as she could. She pushed them as far behind her grandfather's things as possible. She wanted to make sure they would not be found. Then she looked carefully around the room and asked, "Where am I to sleep, Grandfather?"

"Wherever you like," he answered.

Heidi was delighted and began at once to check out every nook and corner. On the wall near her grandfather's bed, she saw a short ladder. She climbed up and found herself in a hayloft. There was a large heap of fresh, sweet-smelling hay. There was also a round window in the wall.

"I shall sleep up here, Grandfather," she called down to him. "It's lovely up here. Come up and see how lovely it is!"

"Oh, I know all about it!" he called up.

"I am getting my bed ready now," she called down again. "I am going to need a sheet."

"All right," her grandfather said. He went to the cupboard and spent a few minutes digging around before he came out with a long, rough piece of material that would have to do for a sheet.

The two worked together to shape the hay into a child-sized bed. They spread the material over the hay, tucking it in until it looked tidy and comfortable.

"The only thing left is a cover," Heidi said. She smiled at her cozy new spot.

Her grandfather left the loft and returned a minute later with a large, thick sack.

"Here," he said. "This should work."

When they got the sack spread neatly over the bed, it looked so warm and comfortable that Heidi squealed with delight.

"This bed looks so lovely! I wish it were night so I could get inside at once."

"I think we should have something to eat first," her grandfather said. "What do you think?"

In the excitement of bed making, Heidi had forgotten everything else. But now she felt terribly hungry.

When lunch was over, Grandfather went outside to put the goat shed in order. Heidi watched him sweep it out and put in fresh straw for the goats to sleep on. She played along the mountainside while the old man did his chores.

The time until evening passed happily. Heidi was skipping and dancing around the tall trees when she heard a shrill whistle. She and her grandfather watched as the goats came springing down from the mountaintops. Heidi sprang forward to greet all of the goat friends she had made that morning. Two of the beautiful, slender animals—one white and one brown—ran to where Grandfather was standing.

"Are they ours, Grandfather? Are they both ours?" Heidi giggled and jumped around with glee.

"The white one is named Little Swan and the brown one is Little Bear," he answered. "Now help me feed these hungry animals."

Heidi helped feed them and send them to sleep. Then she quickly finished her own dinner. She was anxious to try out her new bed. Soon Heidi was sleeping sweetly and soundly. She knew nothing of the strong winds outside that caused the wooden beams of the hut to groan and creak with anger. Her dreams kept away the haunting sounds of branches snapping among the trees.

In the middle of the night the old man got up. "The child will be frightened," he murmured softly to himself. He climbed the ladder to the loft and stood by Heidi's bed.

In the little bit of moonlight left, he could see the face of the sleeping girl. She lay under the heavy sheet, her cheeks rosy and her head peacefully resting on her little round arm. She actually had a smile on her face, as if in the middle of a pleasant dream. The old man stood looking down at the child until the moon disappeared behind the clouds and he could see no more.

CHAPTER 4

Out with the Goats

⟡

Heidi awoke the next morning with a smile on her face. She felt so happy in her new home. She remembered all the things that she had seen the day before and was excited to see them again today. She quickly jumped out of bed and ran outside, joyful at the sound of Peter's voice. While Heidi washed and made herself tidy, Grandfather packed a good lunch for her. In minutes she was out on the mountainside with the goats.

"Come along," Peter yelled to Heidi. "Your grandfather gave me orders to watch you!"

Heidi listened to what he said and followed the boy until he slowed to rest his goats. Peter checked on his herd and then fell asleep on the warm ground. Heidi sat near him. Suddenly she heard a loud cry overhead. Lifting her eyes, Heidi saw a bird. It was larger than any she had ever seen before. It had great, spreading wings and was wheeling around and around in wide circles.

"Peter, Peter, wake up!" called out Heidi. "See the great bird! Look! Look!"

Peter got up and they watched the bird together until it disappeared behind the mountaintops.

"Where has it gone?" asked Heidi.

"Home to its nest," said Peter.

"Let's go see!" Heidi answered with glee.

"No!" Peter said firmly. "Even the goats can't climb that high. Stay here while I get lunch."

Heidi frowned, but only for a second. The goats were playing about her and she wanted to join them.

"Tell me their names," she sang to Peter as he placed her bread and cheese before her.

"That one with big horns is Turk. He always wants to ram the other goats. Most of them run when they see him coming. The only one who stays is Greenfinch. She is the little goat there. She's very brave and so quick that Turk often doesn't see her coming."

All of a sudden Peter leaped to his feet and ran after one of the goats. Heidi followed him as fast as she could. They dashed through the middle of the flock and toward the side of the mountain.

By the time Peter reached the mountainside, Greenfinch was leaping in the direction of the cliff. Peter threw himself down and grabbed one of her hind legs. The goat was surprised and began to bleat angrily. She tried to get free and wriggled so much that Peter had to call to Heidi for help.

Heidi ran right up. She saw the danger both Peter and the animal were in and quickly gathered a bunch of sweet-smelling leaves. She held them under Greenfinch's nose, saying, "Come on, Greenfinch! You must not be naughty! Look, you might fall down there and break your leg."

The young animal quickly turned and began to eat the leaves out of Heidi's hand. Meanwhile Peter stood up and took hold of Greenfinch by the band around her neck. Heidi took hold of her other side in the same way. Together they led the wanderer back to where the rest of the flock was feeding peacefully.

Now that they were back to safety, Peter wasted no time in scolding the animal. He lifted his stick as he yelled, ready to give her a good swat as punishment. "No, no, Peter," Heidi cried out. "You must not hit her. See how frightened she is!"

"She needs it," Peter growled and lifted his stick again. Heidi quickly put herself between the boy and the goat. "You have no right to touch her. It will hurt her. Leave her alone!"

Peter looked with surprise at the little girl. He thought about how kind she was. Heidi had given him most of her lunch today just because she thought he looked hungry. No one had ever done such a nice thing for him. And now she wanted to spare this naughty animal. Peter put down the stick.

"I will let her go if you will give me some more of your cheese tomorrow," he said. He was still frowning about the scare the goat had given him.

"You shall have it all, tomorrow and every day," replied Heidi. "I don't want it. And I will give you bread, too—a large piece like you had today. But then you must promise never to hit Greenfinch or any of the other goats."

"All right," said Peter. "It's a deal." And it seemed the boy really did mean to keep his word.

CHAPTER 5

The Visit to Grandmother

⌒

Day after day Heidi spent her time with Peter. They went high into the meadows and among the rocks and the flowers. When the weather finally grew cold and Grandfather told Heidi to stay home, Peter felt the same unhappiness as the young girl. Not only did he miss the extra food at lunchtime, but he always had more trouble with the goats on those days. The animals seemed to behave better when their kind Heidi was around to guide them.

When it grew *very* cold, Peter no longer took the goats out. This was his time to go to school.

Heidi loved to ask him questions about his schooling, but Peter wasn't fond of answering the girl. He liked his job as a goatherder far more than he liked school. One evening he gave Heidi a message instead of answering her questions.

"Grandmother sent word that she would like you to come and see her," the boy said.

It was quite a new idea for Heidi that she would go visit anyone. For the next few days she bothered Grandfather so much about going that he finally gave in to her wishes.

Grandfather rose from the table. He climbed up to the hayloft and brought down the thick sack to wrap the young girl in. Then he went to the shed and came out dragging a large sled. After climbing into the seat, he placed the girl comfortably on his lap. They took off like a bird gliding swiftly through the air. Within minutes they sailed to a stop in front of Peter's hut.

"There you are now. Go on in. When it begins to get dark you must start on your way home again." Then he left her and went back up the mountain, pulling his sled behind him.

Heidi opened the door of the hut and stepped into the small dark room. It had a fireplace and looked like a kitchen. In the corner sat an old woman, bent over from age. She was spinning wool into yarn on a big spinning wheel. Heidi walked up to her.

"Good day, Grandmother," she said. "I have come at last. Did you think I would never get here?"

The old woman raised her head and felt for the hand that the child held out to her. "Are you the child who lives at the top of the mountain? Are you Heidi?"

"Yes, yes," answered Heidi "I came down in the sled with Grandfather."

"Is it possible? Why, your hands are quite warm! What does she look like, Brigitta?" the old woman asked her daughter, who was sewing in the corner of the room.

"She is a beautiful little girl, much like her mother was. And I believe her grandfather must be taking care of her! She looks quite well!" the younger woman said.

During this time Heidi had not been standing still. She had been wandering around the room, looking carefully at everything there was to see. All of a sudden she exclaimed, "Grandmother, one of your shutters is flapping back and forth. Grandfather will come and make it right for you. See how it keeps banging?"

"Dear child," said the old woman. "I can't see, but I can hear. There are many things wrong with this house. It creaks and rattles so much that I lie awake at night thinking the whole place may just fall down. There is no one to fix it for us. Peter doesn't know such things."

"Why can't you see the shutter?" Heidi asked.

"Heidi, dear, I can't see anything."

"But if I take you out into the snow, there will be more light. Surely you will see it then."

"No, my dear. It is always dark for me now. Whether in the snow or the sun, no light can help me."

Heidi wouldn't give up. "But in the summer, Grandmother, when the hot sun is shining down, it will be bright and beautiful for you again."

"Oh, child, I won't ever see the sunshine gleaming on the mountains or the yellow flowers again."

At these words, Heidi broke into loud crying. In her sadness she kept saying, "Why can't someone make it light for you? Why can't you see?"

Grandmother tried to calm the girl, but it was not easy to quiet her. Heidi didn't cry often. When she did, she could not get over her sadness for a long while.

At last Grandmother said, "Come here, my Heidi. Tell me how Grandfather is. Tell me what you do up there. I knew him very well in the old days, but I have heard nothing of him for many years now. All I know I learn from Peter, who never says much."

This brought a new and happy idea to Heidi. She quickly dried her tears and said, "Wait until I have told Grandfather everything. He will make it light for you again. I am sure of it. And he will fix your house for you, too. He will put everything right."

Grandmother was silent. Heidi began the lively tale of her life with Grandfather and the days she spent on the mountain with the goats. She told Grandmother what fine care the old man took of her and all about the beautiful woodworking he did around the house.

Grandmother listened carefully. Both she and her daughter looked surprised at the wonderful things Heidi was saying about the old man. The young girl talked until the door burst open.

"Peter!" she cried when she saw the boy.

Peter's smile was as big as the girl's. He laughed as she danced about him in glee.

"Peter," Grandmother said quickly. "How is your reading getting on?"

"Just the same," was Peter's answer.

"I had hoped he would be reading by now," Grandmother told Heidi. "There is an old prayer book on the shelf. It has beautiful songs in it that I have not heard for a long time. I can no longer remember them to repeat to myself. I hoped that Peter would soon learn enough to read one of them to me.

"But wait," the old woman continued. "How can you be home so soon? Surely the afternoon hasn't passed by so quickly!"

"Oh, but it has. And it's getting dark," said Heidi sorrowfully. "I promised Grandfather that

I would start back at the first sign of night. I must go!"

Heidi gave Peter a smile and picked up her coat. The old woman made a fuss about the child going out into the freezing air. Finally she sent Peter along to make sure Heidi made it up the mountain. They hadn't gone far before Grandfather met them on the path.

Heidi immediately began telling him about her afternoon visit. "Grandfather, tomorrow we must take the hammer and the long nails. We have to fasten Grandmother's shutter and do some other work. Her house shakes and rattles all over."

"We must, must we? Who told you that?" asked her grandfather.

"Nobody told me," said Heidi. "But Grandmother lies awake at night and trembles with fear that the house will fall on their heads. Everything is dark now for Grandmother and she doesn't think anybody will be able to make it light again. But I am sure you will be able to, Grandfather. Think how awful it is for her to always be in the dark and to be frightened about what may happen. No one else can help her. Tomorrow we must go and make things right. We will, won't we, Grandfather?"

The child was clinging to the old man and looking at him in such a trusting way. He looked down at Heidi for a long while without speaking and then said, "Yes, Heidi, we will do something to stop the rattling. At the very least we can do that. We will go tomorrow."

Grandfather kept his promise. Each day he went and fixed something new. And so the winter went by. After many years of joyless life, Grandmother at last had something to make her happy. Her days were no longer filled with weariness and darkness. She now could look forward to Heidi's visits.

CHAPTER 6

Two Visitors

~⌒∽

If the winter passed quickly, the summer passed
even faster. Now another winter was coming to an
end. Heidi was still as happy as she had been the day
she arrived. She was now eight years old. She had
learned all kinds of useful things from her grandfather. Heidi knew how to look after the goats as
well as anyone, but children her age were supposed
to be in school. The schoolmaster from the town
of Dorfli had already written to her grandfather
about this twice. The old man had sent word back
each time that he would not be sending Heidi to

school. Finally the pastor climbed the mountain to talk with Grandfather about his choice.

"The child should have been in school a year ago," the pastor said. "She is not a goat or a bird. She is a child. It is time for her to begin her lessons. Next winter she must go."

"Indeed," growled Heidi's grandfather. "Do you really wish me to send a young child like that some miles down the mountain through storm and snow? Should I let her return at night when the wind is raging? Even I would run the risk of being blown down and buried in the snow!"

"You are quite right, neighbor," said the pastor in a friendly tone of voice. "I agree that it would be impossible to send her from here. But you must think of the child. It is time to come down from the mountaintop and live among your fellow men. It is too dangerous to live up here. Heidi would not survive if anything were to happen to you in the winter months!"

"Let me assure you, sir, that I take very good care of the child. She stays warm here. My fire never goes out. As for going to live in town, the people there hate me. And I hate them. It is best that we stay away from each other."

"No," said the pastor. "It is not best for you. The people down there do not hate you like you think. You need to make your peace with God and move down with us. You will see how happy you can be."

The pastor stood and raised his hand. "I am sure you will make the right decision. I know that next year we will be neighbors once again. Give me your hand and promise me that."

Grandfather gave the pastor his hand and answered him calmly. "I know you are only thinking of what is best for the child, but I am telling you now that I will not send her to school and I will not move down the mountain to live among the people."

"Then I hope God will help you!" said the pastor. He turned sadly away, left the hut, and went down the mountain.

The pastor's visit left Grandfather in a grouchy mood. When Heidi asked him about going to see Grandmother, he told her, "Not today." Then he didn't speak for the rest of the day. The following morning when Heidi asked about Grandmother again, he answered, "We will see." But before they had even cleared the lunch bowls from the table, another visitor arrived. This time it was Aunt Dete.

Grandfather looked at her fancy clothes without saying a word. He could tell by her face that she was surprised at how well Heidi looked. She was so happy and well cared for that Dete hardly knew her. Leaving the child with her grandfather had always worried Dete a bit, so it was happily that she came to the old man with her wonderful news.

A rich relative of the people she worked for had an only child. The girl was about Heidi's age and had to use a wheelchair to move about. She spent much of her time alone and needed someone to play with her. Dete had talked to the housekeeper about Heidi, and the woman had agreed to take in the little girl. This could be so wonderful for Heidi! She would live in a fancy house and always have someone to play with.

"And who knows," Dete said, "if anything ever happens to the little girl, Heidi might just be lucky enough to—"

"Are you finished with what you came to say?" the old man asked the visitor.

"Ugh!" cried Dete. She threw her hands up in the air. "Anybody else would be thrilled with the news I am bringing you!"

"Then you can take your news to anyone else. I don't want to hear it."

Dete jumped up out of her seat like a rocket. "If you think you can keep my sister's child up here without sending her to church or school, you are mistaken! I am responsible for her! I will not give in!"

"Stop it!" yelled Grandfather. "Leave at once and never let me see you here again!" And with that he left the hut.

"You have made my grandfather angry!" Heidi cried. She looked crossly at Dete.

"He will be fine," the woman said. "Come now, show me where your clothes are."

"I am not coming," said Heidi.

"Nonsense!" Dete said in surprise. "You don't understand things any better than the old man. You will have things you never dreamed of." She went to the cupboard and took out Heidi's things. Then she rolled them in a bundle and handed the girl a hat. "Come along now. This hat is shabby, but it will do for now. Let us go."

41

"I am not coming," repeated Heidi.

"Don't be stupid," Dete answered. "You probably learned how to be stubborn from those goats. Listen to me. You saw how angry your grandfather was. He does not wish to see us ever again. He wants you to go away with me. You shouldn't make him any angrier. Besides, it's so nice where I am taking you. And if you don't like it there, I will bring you back. Your grandfather will be in a good mood by then."

"Can we leave and come back by tonight?" Heidi asked.

"What are you talking about?" Dete asked. "I told you I would bring you back when you want. We will go as far as we can walk today. Then tomorrow we will take the train. It will bring you back again when you want it to—as fast as the wind."

Dete now had the bundle of Heidi's clothes under her arm and the child by the hand. They went down the mountain together.

Heidi heard Peter's voice before she saw the boy. "Where are you going?" he cried. He began to worry when he saw the girl clutching the woman's hand.

"I am just going for a visit to Frankfurt. I will be back." The young girl slowed as she saw Grandmother's hut.

"Oh, I must run in to tell Grandmother. She will be expecting me," said Heidi. She looked up at the woman beside her.

"No, you cannot stop for anyone. When you come back you can bring her a gift."

Heidi was torn between walking down the mountain and running to the hut. She stopped when she heard Grandmother's cry and thought about visiting her for only a minute. But Dete pulled her hand along in such a tight way that the choice was made for her.

CHAPTER 7

A New Family

ℭ

Clara Sesemann was lying on the couch. The girl's legs were weak and it was too hard for her to walk about on her own. Just now she was in the study. This was the room where the family usually gathered. It was easy to see that this was also where Clara took her lessons. A handsome bookcase with glass doors held everything the young girl would need. At the moment, though, she was simply wishing for something to do. Just then she heard visitors at the door.

Her little face was thin and pale. Her soft blue eyes went from the clock to the woman in the room.

"Is it them, Ms. Rottenmeier?" Clara asked softly. She listened for voices in the front hallway.

The lady she was speaking to sat quite still at a small worktable. The housekeeper had been in charge of the girl's care since her mother had died many years before. She was the one Dete had spoken to about Heidi.

Clara was about to ask her question again when Dete and Heidi arrived at the door of the study.

Ms. Rottenmeier looked at Heidi for some minutes. "What is your name?" she asked.

"Heidi," the youngster said softly.

Dete quickly stepped up to change her answer. "Her baptized name is Adelheid, after her mother who is now dead."

Ms. Rottenmeier took a step closer. "I must tell you, Dete, that I am surprised to see a child so young. I told you that I wanted a girl Clara's age. Clara is twelve. How old is Adelheid?"

"I have lost count," Dete answered, trying to hide the truth. "I can't say for sure, but I think she is ten or just about that."

"Grandfather told me I was eight," Heidi chimed in. Dete gave her a poke in the back with her finger.

"What!" Ms. Rottenmeier screamed. "Only

eight? Four years younger! What good will she be? We wanted someone to share school lessons and read books with Clara! What have you even read, child?"

"Nothing," said Heidi.

"What?"

"I never learned to read," Heidi said.

"Mercy!" the older woman cried. "You don't know how to read! Dete, how could you bring me a child like this? You didn't tell me what she was like!"

"Please," Dete answered warmly. "She is a sweet girl, just the kind of companion Clara should have. I must go now, but you will see how wonderfully they get along." With a bow, Dete left the room and ran downstairs. Ms. Rottenmeier stood for a moment not knowing what to do. Then she ran down the steps after the woman. She had too many questions about the child to just let her leave like that.

Heidi stayed by the door. Clara motioned her over and the two began to talk.

"Have you always had that short curly hair?" Clara asked.

"Yes, I think so," said Heidi.

"Are you happy about coming here?" Clara went on.

"No, but I am going home tomorrow," Heidi said. "I am taking Grandmother a gift. I think I will take her a loaf of white bread. Dete says that would be a nice surprise for her."

"You are a funny child," laughed Clara. "You were sent here to live with me and share my lessons, and now I find out you don't even read. We shall have fun with this! My tutor is nice. He will like teaching you as well."

Heidi shook her head and began to say something, but Ms. Rottenmeier came back into the room. She had not been able to catch up to Dete, and the look on her face let Heidi and Clara know she was still angry about it.

"It is time for dinner," she said. Sebastian, the butler, took the girls to the table. While they ate, Tinette, the maid, freshened up the guest room for Heidi.

Ms. Rottenmeier arrived at the table just in time to hear Heidi having a very simple conversation with Sebastian.

"Adelheid, I must make you understand that you are not to speak to any of the help unless you have an order for them." She took the girl's chin and turned it harshly toward her. "Never let me hear you talk to Sebastian in that way again!"

As Ms. Rottenmeier went on with a list of rules that Heidi was to follow in the house, the young girl's eyes slowly closed. She had been up since five o'clock in the morning and had had a long trip through the day. She leaned back in her chair and fell fast asleep.

When Ms. Rottenmeier finally came to the end of her speech, she said, "Now remember what I have said, Adelheid! Do you understand everything?"

"Heidi has been asleep for a long time," said Clara with a huge smile on her face. She couldn't remember when she had had so much fun at dinnertime.

CHAPTER 8

A Look About Town

⁓

W hen Heidi opened her eyes the next day, she
didn't know where she was. As she looked around
the room, she remembered everything that had
happened during the last few days. She jumped
out of bed, got dressed, and ran to the window.
Heidi was eager to see the sky and country outside, but the curtains were too heavy for her to
push aside. Instead, she crept underneath them
to get to the window. But when she got there, she
discovered that the glass was too high. She could
only just get her head above the sill to peer out.

She couldn't see what she wanted. She ran from window to window, finding the same problem at each one. She felt like a caged bird.

All of a sudden Heidi heard someone call, "Breakfast is ready!" She left the window and joined Clara at the dining-room table. Heidi ate her food in a perfect manner. Then when Ms. Rottenmeier wasn't looking, she quickly tucked her white roll into her apron pocket. When the meal was over, she ran upstairs to her room and placed it in the closet to take back to Grandmother. Heidi thought about the day when she could give Grandmother this delicious roll. For now Heidi would try to forget the thoughts about Grandmother. If she didn't, they would make her too sad. With one more look at the roll, she closed the closet door and joined Clara in the den.

As soon as the children were alone, Heidi asked Clara about the windows.

"Oh, you must open the windows to see out.

But they're hard to open. Ask Sebastian to do it for you after our lessons."

∽

When their lessons ended, Clara had to rest for the afternoon. This was Ms. Rottenmeier's time for a break as well, so Heidi was free to do as she pleased. The first thing Heidi did was to seek out Sebastian and have him open a window.

Heidi climbed up onto a stool. At last she was going to see what she had been longing for. But when she looked outside, she found a disappointing view.

"Why, there is nothing outside except for stony streets," she said unhappily. "What would I see if I went to the other side of the house, Sebastian?"

"The same thing," the man said.

"But where can I go to look out over the whole valley?" Heidi asked.

"You would have to climb to the top of a high tower, like that one over there with the gold ball above it. From there you can see everything."

Heidi climbed down from her stool and ran to the street as fast as she could. Things were not as easy as she thought they would be, though. The tower had looked so close from the window. But now she couldn't even tell which direction it was in. She walked slowly through the streets, passing people who all seemed to be in a great hurry to get somewhere. Suddenly she saw a boy standing nearby. He was carrying a hand organ on his back and had a little turtle in his hand. Heidi ran up to him and said, "Where is the tower with the gold ball?"

"I will take you there for four pennies."

Heidi promised she would get the money from Clara later. The young boy seemed to trust her and showed her through the town. Finally they arrived at the tower. They rang the call bell and an old man appeared at the entrance. At first he thought Heidi was too young to be bothered with, but the girl's pleading eyes convinced him to take her to the top of the tower. Heidi held the old man's hand and climbed up the many steps. When they reached the top, the old man lifted her up so that she could look out of the open window.

Heidi saw beneath her a sea of roofs, towers, and chimneys. She drew back her head and said in a small voice, "It's not at all what I thought."

The man set Heidi on the ground and led her back down the narrow stairway. As they turned toward the tower keeper's room, Heidi heard a loud meow.

The little girl stopped and looked about the small area.

Seeing Heidi so interested, the old man pointed her toward a basket.

"Oh, the sweet things, the darling kittens!" she kept on saying.

"Would you like to have one?" asked the old man.

"To keep?"

"Yes, of course. More than one if you like. In fact, you can take them all if you want."

Heidi smiled, thinking of the joy the kittens would bring Clara. "Can I take two today and get the rest later?"

"Of course," the man laughed. "I will even bring them to you!"

Heidi pointed out where she lived. Then the young girl spent a minute or more picking the two kittens that would go with her. She put them in her pockets and scampered down the rest of the steps to the boy waiting on the street.

"Four pennies to take you back?" he said.

Heidi nodded and followed him to her house. Sebastian was waiting at the door.

"Quickly! Quickly, little miss! Go straight into the dining room. Ms. Rottenmeier is waiting for you."

Heidi sprang through the door and Sebastian shut it behind her, leaving the boy standing on the steps.

Heidi walked into the room and listened to Ms. Rottenmeier scold her. When she was finished, she asked Heidi what she had to say for herself.

"Meow," came the answer.

The old lady jumped up in anger. "Adelheid, what did you say?"

"I didn't say—" began Heidi. "Meow, meow!"

Sebastian had a hard time holding in his laughter and almost dropped the dishes. Ms. Rottenmeier stomped to Heidi to see what had made the noise.

"Kittens!" she shrieked. "Sebastian! Tinette! Get those horrible little things out of here! Take them away!" And with that, she turned and went into the den.

Heidi jumped up and ran to Clara. She took

the kittens from her pockets and placed them on the girl's lap.

Clara squealed with delight as she snuggled the kittens to her chest. "Heidi, wherever did you find such dear little things?"

But Heidi was too busy chasing after the scrambling kittens to answer. Her giggles drowned out the orders of Ms. Rottenmeier from the next room. Clara heard the mean shout, though, and knew the woman would do her best to rid the house of these creatures.

"Please, Sebastian, find a place to hide them for us. We must keep them!" Clara begged. She clutched a darling white kitten with a black tip on its tail.

"I will see to it," answered Sebastian with a smile. "I will put them where the lady is not likely to go."

And so Heidi and Clara went to sleep that night knowing that the kittens were safe and warm in a comfortable bed.

CHAPTER 9

Money and Kittens

⌒

The next day the boy returned. He rang the doorbell over and over again until Sebastian answered it.

"What is the meaning of this?" he asked as he flung the door open.

"I want to see Clara," the boy answered.

"What do you want with her?" Sebastian asked roughly.

"She owes me eight pennies," explained the boy.

"You're crazy!" Sebastian laughed.

"She owes me four pennies for showing her the way to the tower and four pennies for showing her the way back."

"You're telling lies! The young lady never goes out. She can't even walk! Leave us alone!" Sebastian tried to close the door.

But the boy was not easily frightened. He remained there and said in a firm voice, "But I saw her in the street. She has short curly black hair, black eyes, and wears a brown dress. She doesn't talk quite like we do."

Uh-oh, Sebastian thought, laughing to himself. *The little miss has been in more trouble.*

"Come inside," he said to the boy.

Sebastian led the way. When they reached the den, he introduced the boy to the girls and the tutor. The boy gave them a half smile, then placed a small turtle he had been holding onto the floor in front of him. The sight of such a strange creature caused the girls to laugh.

It took only a few seconds for Ms. Rotten-meier to appear at the door. "Stop it!" she cried, trying to drown out the girls' giggles.

The children softened their laughter, but Clara couldn't hide her squeals of delight. Sebastian stayed outside, laughing so hard that he almost couldn't stand up. The boy's pet turtle, which he seemed to carry everywhere, was crawling toward the woman's feet. Ms. Rottenmeier jumped onto a chair and began screaming.

"Take them out, boy and animal! Get them away at once!" she ordered.

Sebastian pulled the boy away, grabbing his turtle for him on his way out the door. When they reached the porch, he put something in the boy's hand. "There is the money from Miss Clara. Spend it wisely!" And with that, Sebastian shut the front door.

A few minutes later Sebastian interrupted the lesson again. He stepped into the room and said that someone had brought a large basket. It was to be given to Miss Clara at once.

"For me?" said Clara in surprise. "Bring it to me, please!"

"After your lesson," Ms. Rottenmeier said firmly.

"Oh, but I won't be able to keep my mind on the lesson. I shall just sit and stare at the basket like I am doing right now."

The cover of the basket was loose. At this moment, several kittens came tumbling onto the floor and began racing about the room in every direction.

"Oh, the dear little things! Look how pretty they are!" Clara exclaimed. "Look at this one, Heidi. And look at this one!"

In her delight, Heidi chased the kittens from one corner of the room to the other. The tutor stood by the table, not knowing what to do. Ms. Rottenmeier was so upset that she stood speechless. She watched as the kittens ran about the room and made the girls giggle nonstop. Finally she found her voice and began to yell for Sebastian and Tinette. The two came quickly. Within a few minutes they had the kittens scooped up and back in the basket. They carried them off and put them with the other kittens. Ms. Rottenmeier was left alone with the girls. Instead of yelling, she gave the girls a mean look and left.

By the end of the afternoon Ms. Rottenmeier knew that the day's wild events had been caused by Heidi. The girl had been trouble since the first moment she arrived. Perhaps if Ms. Rottenmeier could make her feel unwanted she would beg to leave.

"Adelheid, I know of only one punishment that will suit what you have done! You are a terrible little girl and I want you to learn that you cannot act like such an animal around us.

Perhaps you will learn your lesson if I put you in a dark cellar with the rats and black beetles."

This last sentence made Clara gasp. "Oh, no, Ms. Rottenmeier. You must wait until Papa comes. He will be home soon. I will tell him everything and he can decide what is to be done with Heidi."

Ms. Rottenmeier could not go against the child's wishes. "Then we shall wait for your father, Miss Clara. But I will be speaking to him as well."

The next few days went by without any major events. Clara had grown much more cheerful since Heidi had moved in. The little visitor added a delightful spirit to the lessons and the routine of the day. She was always trying to get out of her work. She mixed up all of her letters and seemed quite unable to learn them. The tutor tried to draw her attention to their different shapes. He even tried to make her see that this one was like a little horn or that one was like a bird's bill. But this only excited Heidi and she would suddenly call out something silly like, "That is a pigeon! That is a goat!" The tutor tried all different ways to help Heidi remember her letters, but nothing seemed to work. Finally he decided that she must simply be unable to learn the alphabet.

In the meantime Heidi was growing restless. She had been in Frankfurt for a week and now spent most of her time picturing the mountain. The leaves would soon be turning green and the yellow flowers would be shining in the sun. At times Heidi was so homesick that she could hardly stand it. Finally one day she felt she could take it no more. She ran to her room and tied up all the rolls she had been saving for Grandmother. She spent several minutes searching for her hat before finally going downstairs without it. When she reached the front door, she met Ms. Rottenmeier returning from a walk.

"Where are you going dressed like that?" the lady asked. She frowned at the tattered red shawl she had forgotten to throw out. "You know you are not permitted to leave the house!"

"I am going home," said Heidi in a soft voice.

"Going home! You want to go home? You have the best of everything here. Why would you want to leave? You ungrateful child! Why ever would you do such a thing?"

Heidi couldn't help but answer the woman. "I want to go home because Grandmother is waiting for me. If I stay any longer, Greenfinch will get beaten because I won't be there to give Peter any cheese. And I will never get to see the nest where the great bird lives up on the rocks and—"

"Stop with such talk!" Ms. Rottenmeier cried. Then she turned and went up the steps. Along the way, she ran into Sebastian.

"Bring that unhappy little creature in at once!" she ordered. "She is speaking nonsense! And get rid of that red shawl!"

"Got in trouble again?" Sebastian asked as he reached for Heidi.

The little girl put her head down. Tears were beginning to sting her eyes. "There, there," the man said. "Don't let her make you unhappy. You have not cried once in the week that you've been here. Most girls your age would have cried a dozen times by now. Let's put your things back and go see the kittens."

Heidi gave a little nod, but Sebastian knew something in the young girl's heart was breaking. It was easy to see at dinner when she ate no food and in her broken spirit the next day when her lessons began.

Ms. Rottenmeier paid no attention to the girl's change in mood. She only worried that someone might see her in her worn-out clothes or that she may begin acting crazy. It was her job to take care of these problems.

The woman spoke to the tutor about Heidi, and he promised her that there was no need to worry. The girl was a bit strange, but in time she would be fine. She just needed to spend more time around Miss Clara and get a proper education.

As for her appearance, Ms. Rottenmeier knew it was her duty to clean the girl up a bit. With Mr. Sesemann due home in a day or two, he would expect to see the visitor well cared for. The rags she was in simply wouldn't do. Heidi was only a dress size or two smaller than Clara. Ms. Rottenmeier would have a few of the older girl's fine garments snipped and fitted to be right for Heidi. Then the three dresses she came with could be thrown away.

When Heidi heard these plans, the feelings of hope that she would soon be leaving began to fade away. She flung herself down on Clara's couch and broke into a fit of weeping. She sobbed until the tears would come no more. Perhaps things would look brighter when Mr. Sesemann arrived in the morning. Perhaps he would understand why she wanted to go home.

CHAPTER 10

Another Grandmother

News of Mr. Sesemann's expected return brought a great deal of commotion to the house. Clara, of course, was more excited than anyone else. Even though his stay would only be for a few days, she knew her father would spend every extra minute he had with her. She couldn't wait for him to meet Heidi. She knew that he would enjoy the girl's ways every bit as much as she did.

The first thing Mr. Sesemann did when he got home was find his Clara. She and Heidi were in the study. Father and daughter greeted each other with hugs and kisses. The two were deeply attached to each other. Then Mr. Sesemann held out his hand to Heidi. "And this is our little Swiss girl. Come and shake hands with me!"

Heidi gave him her hand and a smile.

"Now tell me, are you and Clara good friends with each other? Or do you get angry and cry and make up and fight again the next day?"

"Oh, no. Clara is always kind to me," answered Heidi.

"And Heidi has never tried to argue," Clara said quickly.

"I am glad to hear it," Mr. Sesemann said as he rose from his chair. "I want my lunch now. I haven't eaten all day. But I will see you right after! Perhaps with a few gifts even!"

୧

Mr. Sesemann did take quite a liking to Heidi,

despite the way Ms. Rottenmeier described the last several days. In fact, he told the woman that he planned to keep Heidi around. She had a pleasant personality and was a wonderful friend for his Clara. He also told Ms. Rottenmeier to treat the child kindly. She shouldn't punish her for the silly things that happened when she was around. If the lady found Heidi too difficult to handle, Mr. Sesemann would hire another person to help her out. In fact, Clara's grandmother would be showing up in a few days for a nice long visit. He was sure she would be a great help when it came to working with the girls.

Mr. Sesemann was only home for a short time before he had to leave for Paris. Clara was sad, but filled with excitement about her grandmother's arrival. She talked about her grandmother so much that soon Heidi also called her Grandmamma. This brought an angry look to Ms. Rottenmeier's face.

"You are not to call her Grandmamma, do you hear me? You must always call her Madam."

Heidi had become so used to the old woman's nasty looks that she just nodded and moved on. Ms. Rottenmeier's scolding no longer upset her.

By the morning of Grandmamma's arrival, Heidi was just as excited as Clara. Both girls screamed and giggled when the carriage pulled in. Sebastian rolled Clara outside to meet Grandmamma. Meanwhile, Heidi waited to be called down from her bedroom. She didn't have to wait long before Tinette popped her head in and told her to go to the study.

As she entered the room, Heidi heard a kind voice say, "Ah, here comes the child! Come over here and let me have a look at you!"

Heidi walked up to the woman and said in a sweet voice, "Good evening, Mrs. Madam."

"Well!" said the grandmother, laughing. "Is that how they talk on the mountain?"

"No," replied Heidi. "I thought that was your name."

"Never mind, sweet child. When I am with children, I am always Grandmamma. You won't forget that name, will you?"

"Oh, no," Heidi answered.

"And what is your name?" Grandmamma asked.

"I am always called Heidi, but here I must be called Adelheid."

"If you have always been Heidi, then Heidi it shall be," Grandmamma said. This bothered Ms. Rottenmeier, who had just walked in the room.

For the rest of the evening, the old woman fussed over the two girls. The following day while Clara was taking her afternoon rest, Grandmamma spent some time talking to Heidi. Ms. Rottenmeier had told her that Heidi couldn't learn like normal children. The tutor couldn't even get her to learn her alphabet.

"Look at these," the woman said to Heidi. She handed the girl a small pile of colorful books.

At first Heidi smiled with delight. But then she opened the second book and let out a cry. For a moment or two she just stared at it. Then the tears begin to fall. At last she burst into sobs.

Grandmamma looked at the picture carefully. It was a green pasture filled with young animals. Some were grazing while others nibbled at the shrubs. In the middle was a shepherd looking at his happy flock.

"Don't cry, dear child," she said. "I will read this story to you later. It really is a very joyful story. There is no sadness in it at all."

It took some time before Heidi could control her sobs. Grandmamma decided to change their talk to something other than the book's picture.

"How are your lessons going, Heidi? Have you learned a lot?"

"Oh, no," replied Heidi. "It is impossible for me to learn."

"Why?" the old woman asked.

"Because reading is too hard for me," Heidi answered.

"Who told you that?" Grandmamma asked with surprise.

"Peter told me, and he knows for sure. He tried and tried and couldn't learn."

"Oh, Heidi, you mustn't go by what Peter says. You have to decide for yourself. I am certain that you would do well if you tried your best."

Heidi shook her head.

"Listen to what I have to say," continued Grandmamma. "You have not been able to learn your alphabet because you believed what Peter said. But now you must believe what I tell you. You can learn to read in very little time. And listen to this—you see the picture with the shepherd and the animals? You shall have that book for your very own just as soon as you are able to read it. Then you will know the story and see how happy it is. You would like that, wouldn't you?"

Heidi listened eagerly to the grandmother's words. "Oh, if only I could read now!"

"It won't take you long to learn," Grandmamma answered. "We will work together."

A few weeks later the tutor came to Grandmamma with a pleasing report. "It is indeed a wonder!" he said. "It is more than I had hoped for. The young lady has learned to read!"

After leaving the tutor, Grandmamma went to find Heidi. Sure enough, the young girl was sitting beside Clara and reading to her. That same day Heidi found the large book with the beautiful pictures lying on her lunch plate. When she looked at Grandmamma, the old woman said, "Yes, it's yours now."

"Mine to keep always—even when I go home?" Heidi asked, blushing with pleasure.

"Yes, of course. It is yours forever," the grandmother said. "Tomorrow we will begin to read it."

～

Heidi's lessons started to go better, but that was the only good change in the young girl. Ever since Ms. Rottenmeier had told Heidi that she was being nasty for wanting to leave, Heidi had lost her spirit. She finally understood that she wouldn't be going home anytime soon. In fact, maybe she would never get to go home. But to share her sadness with Clara or Grandmamma would seem ungrateful. And so the feeling of heaviness on her little heart grew until she could no longer eat. She lay awake at night for hours. As soon as she was alone, the picture of the mountain with its sunshine and flowers would rise before her eyes. When she woke in the morning, she would think she was back at

Grandfather's ready to greet the goats in the morning sun. Her looks of sadness worried Grandmamma.

"Tell me, Heidi," the old woman said, "what is the matter? Are you in trouble?"

Heidi was afraid that Grandmamma would think poorly of her if she told the truth. She didn't want the woman to dislike her, so she simply said, "I can't tell you."

"Then you must speak to God about it. If you can't tell a person, then tell your problems to God. Pray to him to help you."

"I never say prayers anymore," answered Heidi.

"Do not tell me that, Heidi! Why have you stopped?"

"It's no use! God doesn't listen. I have prayed for the same thing every day for weeks and God has not done what I asked." The young girl put her head down.

"You are wrong, Heidi. You must not think of him like that. God is good to all of us. He knows what we need better than we do. And just because he thinks it is better not to give you what you want right now doesn't mean he isn't answering you. You shall have what you ask for, but not until the right time comes."

"I will go right now and ask God to forgive me," Heidi said.

"Go, child. He will help you and give you everything that will make you happy again."

Heidi ran out of Grandmamma's room and into her own. She sat herself on a stool, folded her hands together, and told God about everything that was making her so sad. She begged him to help her and let her go home to Grandfather. She didn't think she could take much more. She just missed home too much.

CHAPTER 11

A Ghost in the House

At last the day came for Grandmamma to leave. It was a sad time for Clara and Heidi. Weeks passed and the only cheer Heidi knew was the book she read in her room each night. Her hopes of seeing Grandfather and the rest of the mountain seemed to fade a little more each day.

Meanwhile, something strange and mysterious was going on in the Sesemann house. Every morning when the servants went downstairs, they found the front door wide open. Nobody in the house knew why. At first they thought there must be a thief sneaking in, but nothing was missing. The servants checked that the door was locked twice a night. Sebastian even put a wooden bar across it for extra safety, but that did no good, either. The next morning, the door was always open again.

The servants took turns trying to solve the mystery. But one by one the adults grew more helpless and less brave. Were strangers trying to break in at night? Were ghosts or other spirits roaming the house? Finally Ms. Rottenmeier couldn't take it any more and decided to write a letter to Mr. Sesemann. The letter told of strange things around the house and explained how frightened she and everyone had become. She also told him that Clara was extremely upset over the ghost. In truth, however, Clara and Heidi found the ghost story quite silly.

The letter was successful, and Mr. Sesemann came home two days later. He talked to the girls and to all the servants in the house. Soon after, he called his friend, the doctor.

"There is no one sick in the house," he told the man when he arrived. "Much worse than that, my friend. We have a ghost!"

The doctor laughed aloud.

"I see you feel bad for us," Mr. Sesemann continued.

"Really, Sesemann, a ghost?"

"I know, I know. I have doubts myself." Mr. Sesemann told him how the front door had been opened each night. Either someone was playing a joke on the servants or there really was a thief.

Finally the doctor agreed to help. Near midnight the two men settled down in armchairs and began talking about all sorts of things. They laughed off the talk of ghosts and chatted happily of old times.

Suddenly the doctor lifted his finger.

"Hush! Sesemann, do you hear something?"

They both listened. They were sure they heard someone lift the wooden bar off the door and put the key into the lock. Mr. Sesemann got up slowly.

"Who's there?" the doctor yelled as he stood up. The two men stepped forward with lights.

The small figure they saw turned and gave a low cry. There in her little white nightgown stood Heidi. Her feet were bare and her eyes were wild. She was trembling from head to foot like a leaf in the wind. The two men looked at each other in surprise.

"Child, what do you need? Why did you come down here?" Mr. Sesemann asked.

Heidi was white with fear and hardly able to make her voice heard. "I don't know," she said.

The doctor stepped up to the child. "This child is sick, my friend. Let me take her to her room."

With that, he put down his light, took the child's hand, and led her upstairs. "Don't be frightened. It's all right. Let's go quietly."

When he reached Heidi's room, the doctor took Heidi in his arms and laid her on the bed. He carefully covered her up and then sat down beside her to wait until she had stopped trembling. Then he took her hand and said in a kind, soothing voice, "There, there, now you feel better. Tell me where you were trying to go."

"I didn't want to go anywhere," said Heidi. "I didn't know I went downstairs, but all at once I was there."

"I see. And were you dreaming?"

"Yes. I dream every night, and always about the same things. I think I am back with my grandfather. I hear the wind in the fir trees outside and I see the stars shining so brightly. I quickly open the door and run out. It's all so beautiful! But when I wake up, I am still in Frankfurt." Heidi struggled to keep back the sobs that seemed to choke her.

"Do you have pain in your head or your back?" the doctor asked.

"No, only a feeling like a big stone is on top of me."

The doctor frowned. "Like you ate something that won't go down?"

"No," Heidi answered, "not like that. It's like I want to cry very much."

"I see," the doctor said. "Do you cry a lot?"

"Oh, no," Heidi said. "Ms. Rottenmeier told me I am not allowed to cry."

"So you just swallow your cry rather than let it come out?" the doctor asked.

"Yes."

"And where did you live with your grandfather?"

"Up on the mountain."

"Wasn't that rather dull and boring?" the man asked.

"Oh, no. It was beautiful!" Heidi could not speak anymore. The tears began to fall fast and she broke into wild weeping.

The doctor stood up and laid her head down on the pillow. "There, there. Go on crying. It will do you good. Then go to sleep. It will all be better tomorrow."

He left the room and went downstairs to Mr. Sesemann.

"Your little one is a sleepwalker. She is the ghost who opened the front door and put fear in your household. The child is homesick. We must do something at once. There is only one cure for this. She must be sent back to her mountain. The girl must leave here tomorrow."

Mr. Sesemann got up and walked back and forth across the room.

"What!" he exclaimed. "The child is a sleepwalker and sick? This all took place in my house and no one saw it? Do you mean, Doctor, that this child came here happy and healthy and I am to send her back to her grandfather a miserable, sick little girl? I can't do it! Make the child well and then we shall send her back."

"Sesemann," replied the doctor, "think of what you are saying. You can't fix the girl with medicine. This child is strong. If you send her back at once, she may get better in the mountain air. But if you wait, she may not get better at all."

Mr. Sesemann stood still. The doctor's words were a shock to him.

"If you put it that way, Doctor, then there is only one choice. She shall leave tomorrow." Mr. Sesemann and the doctor walked up and down for a while figuring out what to do next. The doctor left just as the morning light was beginning to creep into the house. The plans for Heidi's trip home had been made.

CHAPTER 12

Heading Home

⟨∽⟩

Mr. Sesemann raced through the house. He banged on doors and called to the servants. Even though it was only four o'clock in the morning, it was easy to see that he wanted every one in the house to wake up.

Ms. Rottenmeier woke from her sleep with a cry of fear. She heard the master calling that she was to get dressed and meet him in the dining room. She thought it had something to do with the ghost that they all had been worried about. It wasn't until several minutes later that the woman found out what the meeting was actually for.

"We are preparing for a journey," Mr. Sesemann said. He was in good spirits. "John, get the horses and carriage ready. Tinette, go wake Heidi and get her dressed for her trip. Sebastian, hurry off to the house where Dete works and bring her here. Ms. Rottenmeier, get out a trunk at once. Pack up all the things that belong to the Swiss child. Add a bundle of Clara's things as well so that the girl might go home with some nice-looking clothes. But do it now!"

Ms. Rottenmeier simply stood still and stared straight ahead. She had expected some long story about a ghost, which she surely would have enjoyed now that it was daylight. Instead she had been given these strange directions. She was still starry-eyed when Mr. Sesemann left to go see Clara.

As he expected, the poor girl was very upset at the idea of her friend leaving. But as she listened to her father's words, Clara understood that they were only doing what was best for Heidi.

"Please, Papa, don't let her leave until I have packed some special things in her box."

Clara's father smiled and winked to let her know that this would be fine. In the meantime, Dete came and Mr. Sesemann told her about Heidi. He asked Dete to take the girl home to her grandfather. But the young woman remembered how the old man had thrown her out of his house. She did not want to face him again! She told Mr. Sesemann that she was much too busy at her job to get away right now.

Mr. Sesemann said he understood. He sent Dete on her way and called for Sebastian. He would deliver the girl. Mr. Sesemann gave him a letter for Heidi's grandfather that would explain everything.

Meanwhile, Heidi was standing quietly to the side. She was dressed in her Sunday best, waiting to see what was going on. Tinette had woken her, but had not told her why. When Mr. Sesemann met her at the breakfast table, he looked eagerly into her eyes and said, "What do you think of all this, little one?"

Heidi gave him a puzzled look.

"Why, you don't know anything about it, I see," laughed Mr. Sesemann. "You are going home today. Going at once!"

"Home?" murmured Heidi in a low voice.

"Don't you want to hear more about it?"

"Oh, yes, yes!" cried Heidi. For the next several minutes, the young girl couldn't tell if she was awake or dreaming. She tried to listen to Mr. Sesemann, but all she could think about was Grandmother and her grandfather and Peter and the goats and the mountain and . . .

Clara sent for Heidi and filled her box with a list of things. There were dresses, aprons, handkerchiefs, and all kinds of material.

"And look here," she added as she held up a basket. Heidi peered in and jumped for joy. Inside were twelve beautiful white rolls for Grandmother. In their delight, the children forgot that the time had come for them to part. When someone yelled that the carriage was ready, there was no time for sadness.

Heidi ran to get her favorite book—the one Grandmamma had given to her. She knew no one would have packed it because it was under her pillow. She put the book in the basket with the rolls. Then she opened her closet to look for another treasure that no one would have thought to pack—the old red shawl she had brought with her. The little girl wrapped it around a stuffed kitten Clara had made for her and put it on top of the basket. Then she put on her hat and left the room. As she climbed into the carriage, she gave Clara her best wishes and thanked Mr. Sesemann for his kindness. She also asked him to send her thanks along to the doctor. She knew she would not be going home if it weren't for him and his promise of *It will all be better tomorrow.*

The carriage started moving and Heidi was off. She held her basket tightly on her lap. For many hours she sat as still as a mouse. She was afraid to move for fear that she might wake up from a dream. She couldn't believe she was finally going home.

When they finished the train ride, Sebastian hired a horse and cart to take Heidi as far as possible. She would finish the rest of the journey on foot. The young girl assured him that she could easily find her way up the mountain. Her grandfather would fetch her trunk later. Sebastian took her aside and gave her the letter for her grandfather. He also gave her a small package, which he said was a present from Mr. Sesemann. She was to put both of these things under the rolls in the basket so she wouldn't lose them. Sebastian waved and watched the smiling girl ride off.

When they got to the village, Heidi jumped off the cart, told the driver that her grandfather would send for the trunk, and began climbing the steep path up the mountain.

It seemed like hours, but at last Heidi caught sight of Grandmother's house. Her heart began to beat louder and she ran faster and faster. She trembled as she reached for the door.

"Oh, my!" said a voice from inside. "That is how my Heidi used to run in here. If only I had her with me once again."

"It's me, Grandmother!" cried Heidi. She ran and flung her arms about the woman. Tears of joy ran down the old woman's cheeks.

"Yes, yes, that is her hair and her voice. Thank you, God! You have answered my prayers!" Tears of joy fell from the blind eyes and landed on Heidi's hand. "Is it really you, Heidi? Have you really come back?"

"Yes, Grandmother, I am really here," answered Heidi. "Don't cry. I am really here." And with that, the child pressed the old woman's hands to her cheeks. It was a feeling she had missed over and over again during the past few months.

CHAPTER 13

Home at Last

⁓

Heidi spent only enough time at Grandmother's to make sure she was well and to give her a few of the white rolls she had been carrying so carefully.

"I've never tasted better," the old woman said as she bit into a roll. "But the real treat is having you back."

Heidi gave the old woman one last hug and promised to come by again tomorrow. Right now she wanted to get home to Grandfather. To be so close and not see him was almost more than the little girl could bear.

Heidi climbed the mountain so fast that she reached her grandfather's hut in a matter of minutes. Before the old man had time to see who was coming, Heidi rushed up to him, threw down her basket, and flung her arms around his neck. She kept saying over and over, "Grandfather, Grandfather!"

The old man said nothing. For the first time in many years his eyes were wet and he had to wipe them. He loosened Heidi's arms and put her on his knee. He looked at her for a moment and then said, "So you have come back to me, Heidi. Did they send you away?"

"Oh, no, Grandfather!" Heidi said.

She spent the next several minutes telling him all about Clara and Mr. Sesemann. She gave him the letter and watched as he read it.

"He has given you enough money to buy a bed and clothes to last you for many years."

"I don't need it, Grandfather. I have a bed already. And Clara put a lot of clothes in my box. I'll never need any more."

"Put it in the cupboard then," the old man said. "I'm sure you will want it someday."

Suddenly Heidi heard a shrill whistle outside. She darted out like a flash of lightning. "Little Swan! Little Bear! Do you remember me? Hello, Peter!"

Heidi was out of her mind with delight at being among her old friends again. Everything was as it should be. It was with a happy heart that Heidi lay down that night. Her sleep was sounder than it had been in months. Grandfather got up at least ten times during the night and climbed the ladder to see if Heidi was all right. But Heidi didn't stir. She didn't have to worry about that burning in her heart. She had heard the wind in the fir trees. She was at home again on the mountain.

The next morning Grandfather went down the mountain to fetch Heidi's trunk. The young girl walked with him as far as Grandmother's cottage, then gave a wave and skipped to the door.

Grandmother could hardly wait to tell Heidi how much she had enjoyed the white roll and how much stronger she felt after eating it. Peter's mother told Heidi that her mother would surely get some of her strength back if only she could eat like that for a week. But she wanted to make the rolls last, so she had only eaten one so far.

Suddenly Heidi smiled. "I have lots of money, Grandmother," she cried. "I know what I will do with it! You must have a fresh white roll every day and two on Sunday. Peter can get them for you!"

"I can't let you do that," the old lady answered. "You give that money to your grandfather. He will tell you how to spend it."

"No, we need to make you strong. We will get you the rolls! Perhaps if you get strong, everything will get light again for you. Maybe it is only dark because you are weak "

As Heidi was jumping about with joy, she noticed Grandmother's songbook. "Oh Grandmother, I can read now! Let me read you a prayer song!"

Heidi beamed with happiness as the old woman's face softened to a look the young girl had never seen.

"You have lightened my heart, dear child," the old woman said when Heidi had finished reading. "Read it again. Just once more."

CHAPTER 14

Sunday Bells

⌒

"Oh, Grandfather," Heidi said as she and the old man walked back up the mountain. "Our lives are happier now than they have ever been before!" She skipped along, swinging the old man's hand. All at once Heidi grew quiet and said, "When I was in Frankfurt, I prayed to come home right away. But if God had let me come at once, then everything would have been different. I would only have had a little bread for Grandmother and I wouldn't be able to read. God has made it all so much better than

I ever could have imagined. It has happened just as Grandmamma said it would. Oh, how glad I am that God did not let me have my way from the start. From now on, I will pray to thank God for what he has done for me. And when he doesn't do what I ask, I shall think to myself, *God has a better plan for me.* We will pray every day, won't we Grandfather? We must never forget him again or else he may forget us."

"And what if we do forget him?" said Grandfather in a sad voice.

"Then everything goes wrong. God lets us go where we like and we get poor and sad. No one feels bad for us because we ran from God and he is the one who would have helped us."

"That is true, Heidi. Where did you learn that?"

"From Grandmamma. She explained it all to me."

They walked on for a while before Grandfather spoke again. "Can we ever go back, Heidi? If we ran from God, are we forgotten forever?"

"Oh, no, Grandfather, we can go back. Grandmamma told me so. And I read the story in my beautiful book. I will read it to you when we get home." Heidi seemed happy with herself and joyfully sang and skipped the rest of the way home. Right before bedtime she read Grandfather the story.

She told him about the man in the picture who was happy at home and went out in the fields with his father's flocks. He was dressed in a fine cloak and stood leaning on his shepherd's staff watching as the sun went down. All at once he wanted to have his own goods and money. He wished to be his own master, and so he asked his father to give him some money. He left his home and soon lost everything. Finally he went back home and told his father, "I am not worthy of you anymore."

His father saw him and ran to him and kissed him. He told his servants to bring him his best robe, a ring for his hand, shoes for his feet, and plenty of food. He said his son was once dead but was now alive again.

"Isn't that a beautiful tale, Grandfather?" said Heidi.

"You are right, Heidi, it is a beautiful tale," he replied. But the old man looked so serious that Heidi grew silent herself.

৵

Early the next morning the old man stood in front of his hut looking at all the beauty.

"Come along, Heidi! The sun is up! Put on your best dress. We are going to church today!"

The two were quite a sight in church. They slipped in after the music had begun. Many people had to look twice before they figured out whom they were seeing. But by the end of the service everyone had seen Heidi and her grandfather.

At the end of church Grandfather took Heidi by the hand and made his way to the pastor's house. The rest of the worshippers stood in small groups. They were all whispering about the man and how gentle he was with Heidi. The cart driver told everyone how Heidi had left the place where she had the best of everything just to be back here with her grandfather. Soon everybody began to feel quite friendly toward the old man.

Meanwhile Grandfather had gone into the pastor's house. They shook hands warmly. The pastor's kind eyes shone with pleasure.

"I have come to ask your forgiveness for the words I spoke to you," Grandfather began. "You were right. It's time to move Heidi off the mountain."

"We will all welcome you as neighbors," the pastor said. And with that, Grandfather stepped outside with Heidi. The door had hardly shut behind him when the whole church group came forward to meet him. There were so many new faces that Grandfather didn't know where to begin. Some even went halfway up the mountain with the old man. They talked about inviting him to lunch and calling on him very soon.

Heidi couldn't believe the softened look on her grandfather's face. "You look nicer today. I've never seen you quite like that before."

"Well, Heidi," he began, "I am happier today than I deserve. Happier than I thought possible. It is good to be at peace with God and my friends. God was good when he sent you to my hut."

When they reached Grandmother's hut, the old man opened the door and walked in with Heidi. "We have some more patching up to do before the autumn comes."

Peter charged through the door and interrupted their talk.

"There is a letter here for Heidi!" he exclaimed.

The letter was from Clara. It said that she and Grandmamma would like to visit Heidi and her grandfather in the coming fall.

There was so much to think about now— the visitors, the move down to Dorfli, the special way that Grandpa seemed to be getting along with others. Life had certainly changed on the mountain, and soon things would be changing even more.

CHAPTER 15

A Visit at Last

❧

Unfortunately, poor health kept Clara from making the journey to the mountain. As disappointed as she was, she did try to do the next best thing. She and her father agreed that sending the doctor for a little vacation would be good not only for Heidi, but for the old doctor as well. The poor gentleman's wife had died some time ago, and his daughter had recently died as well. The doctor had simply not been the same since.

When Mr. Sesemann asked if he would go to the mountains, the doctor said he would be honored. He would take all of the wonderful things Clara had packed for her friends and make sure they got to everyone safely. Clara had chosen gifts for Grandmother and Grandfather and even for Peter.

Meanwhile at Heidi's home, the young girl woke up early every morning. She dressed herself as quickly as she could and went outside to wait. She peered down the mountain as far as she could see. This had been her routine every morning for a week now. She was expecting Clara and Grandmamma any day and she wanted to be ready when they got there.

But instead of Clara, she heard Peter's whistle. "Can you come out with me today?" he asked.

Heidi told her friend that she could not. She was waiting for company. Peter was disappointed, but this morning the wait was worth it.

"Grandfather! Grandfather! Come, come!" Heidi called out. "They are coming! They are coming and the doctor is in front of them!"

Heidi rushed forward to welcome her old friend. The doctor held out his hands to greet her. When she reached him, she clung to his outstretched arms. Then with joy in her heart she said, "Good morning, Doctor, and thank you ever so many times."

"God bless you, child! What have you got to thank me for?" asked the doctor, smiling.

"For sending me home to my grandfather," the child explained.

The doctor's face brightened like a ray of sunshine had passed across it. He thought the young girl would have forgotten him by now. Instead her eyes were dancing for joy. She was full of thanks and clinging to the arm of her old friend.

"Take me to your grandfather, child," the old man said.

"But where are Clara and Grandmamma?"

"I am so sorry, Heidi, but I have come alone. Clara was very ill and could not travel. Grandmamma stayed behind to take care of her. But they will come next spring when the days are warm and long again."

Heidi stood still for a second, allowing the sad news to sink in. "Come along, Doctor," Heidi said. "Let's find Grandfather."

The two men became friends at once. They shared the day on the mountain, planning out the doctor's vacation for the next several weeks. As they sat down to a lunch of milk and toasted cheese, they saw a man coming up the path carrying a large package on his back.

"Ah, the package from Clara," the doctor said and smiled at Heidi.

The young girl's eyes grew bright.

"Open your treasures, Heidi," the doctor said. He pushed the large package toward her.

One by one Heidi pulled out the items Clara had packed so carefully. Cakes and a shawl for Grandmother, some new tools for Grandfather, sausage for Peter, and clothing for herself. The only thing that made Heidi happier than the gifts was seeing the pleasure on the doctor's face. He truly enjoyed seeing Heidi so well and happy again.

CHAPTER 16

Another New Home

⁊

The doctor's stay turned out to be a wonderful time for everyone. Grandfather enjoyed the company of an older gentleman to share stories and spend time with. Heidi took great joy in showing her friend every corner of the mountain. She finally had the chance to prove the beauty she had once only been able to talk about. And the doctor . . . he enjoyed the closeness of good friends and the fresh air and freedom of the mountain. Getting away from the city helped him forget his troubles and enjoy life again.

And so it was a sad day when he finally left. Heidi's heart ached so badly that she sobbed and asked to go along.

"No, no, dear child," the doctor said kindly. "You must stay or you will end up sick again. But if I ever need someone to take care of me, you will be the first person I call. May I do that?"

"Yes," Heidi answered. "I will come the first day you send for me. I love you nearly as much as I love Grandfather."

And so the doctor waved good-bye and started on his way. Heidi looked after him until he became a tiny speck in the distance. As the doctor turned to look back at Heidi and the sunny mountain for the last time, he said to himself, "It is good to be up there . . . good for the body and the soul. A man might learn how to be happy again here."

The rest of the autumn seemed to go slowly for Heidi, for she dearly missed her friend's company. But finally the fresh snow came to the mountain. Grandfather kept his word and moved Heidi and the goats down to Dorfli. There was an old building near the church that had been abandoned for years. Grandfather had worked through the autumn months to make it sound and tight.

Heidi was thrilled with her new home. Living in Dorfli meant that she was able to go to school every morning and afternoon. She worked hard in school and eagerly learned everything that was taught to her. She hardly ever saw Peter there. He said the snow was too deep on the mountain to make it to school. But he always seemed to be able to make his way through the snow to pay Heidi a visit once school was over.

Heidi loved seeing Peter each night, but it made her more and more lonesome for Grandmother. Each time she asked to go visit,

Grandfather told her that the snow was too deep. It wasn't until many winter days went by and the sun appeared again that Heidi was finally able to visit the old woman.

Heidi was surprised to find her in bed rather than in her corner.

"Are you ill, Grandmother?" Heidi asked quickly.

"No, no, child," answered the old woman. "It is just the cold getting to me."

"So you shall be well when it is warm again?"

"Yes. I do so want to get back to my spinning," Grandmother said.

Heidi read to the old woman until it was dark. She could actually see the peacefulness spreading over the old woman as she listened to the words of her hymns. How soothing the verses were to her! It didn't seem long, though, until Peter had to put the girl on the back of his sled to head home. The two of them shot down the side of the mountain like two birds darting through the air.

When Heidi was lying in bed that night, an idea struck her that she could barely wait to share. But it wasn't until Peter came the next day that she told him her thoughts.

"You must learn to read, Peter," she told her friend.

"I can read," he said.

"Yes, but I mean really read so that you can read to Grandmother. You need to read the hymns."

The young girl stared into the boy's eyes. "I will teach you."

"But why?" he asked. "You can read them to her on your visits."

"She needs to hear them every day, Peter. They make her feel so much better. That is a gift that you can give her. I cannot be there for her the way you can."

The young boy put his head down like he was thinking his answer over.

"I will learn if you can teach me," Peter said at last.

A smile spread over Heidi's face. She knew in her heart that he would do just fine.

CHAPTER 17

News from Faraway Friends

⤳

It was a long winter, but finally May came. With Heidi's help, Peter had learned to read quite well. Grandmother now had the joy of hearing a hymn every day. Peter felt good about his learning and decided to go to school more regularly. Heidi had made a difference for both Grandmother and Peter.

The sunshine had also made quite a difference. When the first signs of spring appeared, Heidi and Grandfather moved back to the mountain. The young girl and her grandfather began to prepare for their springtime company at once. It wasn't long before the letter from Clara arrived.

It would be at least six weeks, but the visitors were coming! Clara and Grandmamma could hardly wait.

The time until Clara's visit moved slowly, but finally it passed. Then came the day when a strange-looking parade was seen making its way up the mountain. In front were two men carrying a chair. A girl wrapped up in shawls sat on the chair. Behind her was a woman on a horse with a guide walking beside her. Next was a chair being pushed by another man. Finally there was a gentleman with such a bundle of shawls and furs on his back that it rose well above his head.

"Here they come! Here they come!" shouted Heidi. She jumped with joy. It was indeed the guests from Frankfurt.

Clara and Grandmamma finally reached the hut and were introduced to Grandfather. Before long the four acted like old friends. While Grandfather and Grandmamma prepared the milk and toasted cheese for their meal, Heidi pushed Clara's chair to every spot she had ever described. Finally the group sat down to eat.

"Do I really see you taking a second piece of toasted cheese, Clara?" Grandmamma asked with surprise.

"Oh, it does taste so nice, Grandmamma— better than all the dishes we have at home."

"It's the mountain air!" said Grandfather. "Everything seems better here."

After the meal Heidi showed off the inside of the hut. She saved her bedroom for last.

"It's delightful here, Heidi!" Grandmamma said. "From your bed you can look straight into the sky. Outside the fir trees are waving, and there is such a delicious smell around you.

I have never seen such a pleasant, cheerful bedroom."

"I have been thinking," Grandfather said, "that if you were willing, Clara might remain up here. I am sure she would grow stronger. We would look after her well."

"You are indeed kind. I thank you with my whole heart." Grandmamma took his hand and gave it a long and grateful shake.

For the next half hour, there was much excitement. Grandmamma and Grandfather worked to get things ready. The shawls and blankets that the visitors had brought along made a perfect topping for the hay in Clara's bed. Clara and Heidi were almost too excited to speak. They giggled and watched as the two grown-ups worked carefully to make everything right. A short while later Grandmamma was up on her horse. She waved good-bye to the girls and promised to see them soon.

That night as Clara lay in the hayloft, she looked through the round window and right into the middle of a shining cluster of stars.

"Heidi, it's just as if we were in a high carriage and were going to drive straight into heaven."

"The stars twinkle because they live up in heaven and are happy," Heidi answered. "Then the stars nod at us because they want us to be happy, too. You know, God fixes everything so we don't need to worry. All things will be fine in the end."

The two children sat up, said their prayers, and put their heads down to rest. Clara lay awake for a long time, unable to believe the wonder of the day. She thanked God over and over again for making this day so fine.

CHAPTER 18

Life at Grandfather's

⟡

For the next three weeks life on the mountain was full of excitement. Heidi shared everything with Clara.

"Now you see that it is just like I told you," Heidi said one morning as they lay with the warm sun upon their hands and feet. "It is the most beautiful thing in the world to be up here with Grandfather."

"Oh, Heidi. If only I could stay up here with you forever!" Clara exclaimed happily.

While the girls played, Grandfather did his part to make sure the visitor was well cared for. Since it was the finest they had, he gave her only Little Swan's milk to drink. He made sure she got plenty of food and fresh air, and he worked with her legs. He hoped that she might actually be able to take a step someday.

"Won't the little daughter try to stand for a minute or two?" Grandfather asked. Clara made the effort in order to please him, but she clung to him as soon as her feet hit the ground. She said that it hurt her too much.

The two girls were full of smiles and adventure each morning. It wasn't long before Heidi was begging Grandfather to take them out with the goats. Finally Grandfather agreed. One fine sunny morning he wheeled Clara's chair out of the shed. Then he went inside to call the girls and tell them what a lovely sunrise they were missing.

Peter arrived at just this moment. The goats didn't gather around him as they usually did. It seemed they had taken a disliking to him lately. He had been so angry and mean to them over the last several weeks. The poor goats didn't know that it wasn't them who had made Peter mad. It was Heidi's friend. Because of this girl who couldn't walk, Heidi had quit coming out with Peter. He had lost his friend. His days were now long and lonely, and it was all Clara's fault.

When Peter saw her chair sitting there, he glared at it like it was an enemy. He looked around, but there was no sound anywhere and no one to see him. The boy sprang forward like a wild creature. He caught hold of the chair and gave it an angry push in the direction of the cliff. The chair quickly rolled forward and disappeared.

Pieces of chair flew in all directions. Peter felt such joy at seeing it fly apart that he clapped his hands and jumped over the bushes on his way up the hill. He didn't care that he might get in trouble for his actions. All he knew was that Heidi's friend would have no way to get around. She would have to go home now. With Clara gone, Heidi would be alone and would surely come out with him again.

But even without the chair, Grandfather and the girls went up the mountainside. Grandfather carried Clara and Heidi skipped merrily alongside.

The group found Peter farther up the mountain with the rest of the goats.

"Why didn't you stop for my goats?" Grandfather asked.

"I did, but no one was there," Peter answered. Grandfather became angry and asked him about the chair, but Peter said he didn't know anything.

Grandfather made sure that Clara was sitting

comfortably on a shawl and then left to do some work at home. Heidi and Clara sat amid the clover, enjoying the weather and the beauty of their surroundings.

Some hours went by, and Heidi began to think she couldn't sit still for another moment.

"Would you think me unkind, Clara, if I left you for a few minutes? I would like to see how the flowers are looking. I would run there and back very quickly . . ."

Clara smiled her agreement and Heidi ran off. The field of flowers was more beautiful than the young girl remembered. The deep blue color, the heavenly smell—it was all too wonderful not to share.

"Oh, you must come!" Heidi called back over her shoulder to Clara. "I will carry you!"

The other girl sighed. "Heidi, whatever are you thinking? You're smaller than me! If only I could walk!"

Heidi looked around like she was searching for an idea.

"Peter! Peter!" she called.

The boy came over. Afraid that his young friend may have found out about the chair, he agreed to help with her idea.

"Peter," Heidi began, "put your arm in the shape of a ring. Now, Clara, put your arm through his." Heidi continued to give both of them directions. Finally the young girl who usually sat in a chair with wheels began to walk.

"You can walk now, Clara, you can walk!"

The girls were so excited that they decided to practice walking every day. With each day it got a little easier and Clara was able to go a longer distance. Another week went by and finally the day came when Grandmamma was to come up the mountain for her second visit. The old woman was in for quite a treat. She was sure to be pleased beyond words when she saw her

Clara walk for the first time. The two girls planned to sit on the bench outside the hut. They would wait for Grandmamma to come close enough to see her face and then they would show her their surprise.

CHAPTER 19

Good-bye Until We Meet Again

❧

"Is it really you, dear child?" Grandmamma said as she approached the hut. "Your cheeks have grown round and rosy! Can that be you, Clara?"

Grandmamma nearly ran toward the two girls sitting on the bench.

"Why aren't you in your chair, Clara? You could fall from that . . ."

Heidi and Clara looked at each other and then got up from the bench. The two children began walking toward the surprised woman.

"Clara! My Clara! You are walking!" Laughing and crying, Grandmamma ran to the girls, hugging first Clara and then Heidi. All at once she caught sight of Grandfather standing by the seat. She ran to him and gave the dear old man a hug.

"How much I have to thank you for! This is all your doing! It happened because of your care."

"And God's good sun and mountain air," he added, smiling.

Clara explained how Grandfather had worked with her through the past weeks. She also described how Heidi had spent every minute of her day finding things for them to do. Clara was having the most wonderful time of her life.

Grandmamma couldn't believe the changes that had taken place. They were still talking about them when they saw a figure coming up the hill. It wasn't until he got closer that Clara realized who it was.

"Papa!" she shouted, totally surprised to see him.

Mr. Sesemann stopped suddenly, staring at the two children before him. All at once his eyes filled with tears. What memories arose in his heart. In his Clara's face he could see the woman he had married. Clara had always been too thin, but now she was healthy and looked just like her mother. Mr. Sesemann didn't know if he was awake or dreaming.

"Don't you know me, Papa?" Clara called to him. She was bursting with happiness. "Am I so changed since you last saw me?"

Mr. Sesemann ran to his child and clasped her in his arms.

"Yes, you are indeed changed! How is it possible? Is it true what I see?" The delighted father stepped back to look at her again. He hoped that the sight of her wouldn't disappear before his eyes.

"Are you my little Clara? Really my little Clara?" he kept on saying. Grandmamma came up now, anxious to see her son. "You have given us quite a surprise in coming here, but I think we have given you a better one."

Mr. Sesemann told them that he had gone home only to find that his mother and Clara had left for their visit to the mountain. He thought that it would be a wonderful idea to join them. He had met Peter along the way, and the boy had brought him up the mountain. How glad he was to be there. This was one of the best days of his life. His little girl was actually walking!

The rest of the afternoon brought much happiness for everyone. Clara and her family wanted to show their thanks for all the kindness they had received.

"Peter, you have shared your Heidi with us long enough," Grandmamma said. Peter had felt ashamed earlier and told Grandfather and

Grandmamma about the chair. When he explained how lonely he had been, they had forgiven him right away. After all, this miracle never would have happened had Clara still had her chair.

"You need something pleasant to remember us by," Grandmamma said to the boy. "I know. We will give you money to spend each week."

"For the rest of my life?" the boy asked quickly.

"Yes, for the rest of your life," Grandmamma answered. Mr. Sesemann nodded in agreement and shook the boy's hand. Peter ran off leaping and jumping with joy.

"Now, dear friend," Mr. Sesemann said to Grandfather, "you have given us a gift far greater than we can ever repay. Surely there must be something we can do for you?"

Grandfather thought for a moment. "I am growing old," he began. "I shall not be here much longer. I need to know that my Heidi will be cared for after I am gone."

"That should not even be a worry, my friend," Mr. Sesemann answered. "I look upon the child as my own. We will never allow her to be left in anyone else's care." Grandfather smiled his thanks.

"And what about you, Heidi? Is there anything you wish for?" Grandmamma asked.

Heidi thought for a long time before she answered. "Yes," she said firmly. "I want to have my bed from Frankfurt sent to Grandmother. That way she won't have to lie with her head downhill and she will be warm enough on even the coldest nights."

"How good of you to think of others," Grandmamma said with a hug. "Of course we can do that. And I shall like to meet this wonderful Grandmother."

The visit to Grandmother brought more joy

to the old woman than Heidi had ever thought possible. Just knowing that her Heidi would not be leaving her again was wonderful enough. But to know that she had friends who truly cared about her warmed her heart to no end.

The next morning Clara had to say good-bye to the beautiful mountain. But the summer would come again and by then Clara would be walking better than ever. Her next visit to the mountain would be even more wonderful.

Heidi ran to the far edge of the slope and waved her hand to Clara until the last glimpse of the girl disappeared.

⌒

The bed arrived from Frankfurt a few days later. For the first time in many years, Grandmother had a sound night of sleep. She continued to sleep on the bed and grew stronger with each passing day. Peter and Heidi sat by Grandmother's side and told her tales from the summer. They also described the beauty of the mountainside in the spring, for there is no better place on earth to be.

The doctor came back to town, this time to stay. He fixed up an old house in Dorfli and lived there with Heidi and Grandfather. The house even had a warm stall out back for the two goats to pass the winter months in comfort.

As for the little girl who was brought to the mountain all those years ago, she vowed never to leave its splendor. For Heidi had all the happiness she needed right there on the mountain. Grandfather had given her more than a home when he took her in. He had given her a life filled with love, warmth, and care. It was now her pleasure to share these things with others. For as she knew deep down in her heart, everything always works out in the end.

What Do *You* Think?
Questions for Discussion

୰

Have you ever been around a toddler who keeps asking the question "Why?" Does your teacher call on you in class with questions from your homework? Do your parents ask you questions about your day at the dinner table? We are always surrounded by questions that need a specific response. But is it possible to have a question with no right answer?

The following questions are about the book you just read. But this is not a quiz! They are designed to help you look at the people, places, and events in the story from different angles. These questions do not have specific answers. Instead, they might make you think of the story in a completely new way.

Think carefully about each question and enjoy discovering more about this classic story.

1. Why does Dete leave Heidi with her grandfather? Do you think she was right to do so? Who would you rather have stayed with— Dete or Grandfather?

2. Why do you suppose Dete was so angry at Heidi for removing her clothes on her way up the mountain? Have you ever gotten in trouble for something you didn't know you'd done wrong?

3. Why do you think Heidi and Grandmother enjoy each other's company so much? Is there anyone you love to spend time with?

4. One of the few things that makes Grandmother feel better is listening to someone read

from her prayer book. Why do you suppose this is? What makes you feel better when you're upset?

5. Why do you suppose Dete introduces Heidi as Adelheid? How do you think this makes Heidi feel? Do you have a nickname or a name that you prefer to be called?

6. When Clara sends a package to Heidi, she makes sure to include presents for everyone. What would you have included in the package? Has anyone ever sent you a package like this?

7. Why is Peter jealous of Clara? Do you think he is right to feel this way? Have you ever been jealous of someone?

8. Heidi is a curious girl. Everywhere she goes she asks questions. Have you ever met anyone like Heidi? What are you curious about?

9. Peter and Heidi have very different attitudes about going to school. Do you know

anyone who feels the same way as Heidi? As Peter? Who are you more like?

10. The last lines of the book say that Heidi knew deep down in her heart that everything always works out in the end. Do you agree with this statement?

Afterword
by Arthur Pober, Ed.D.

⌒

First impressions are important.

Whether we are meeting new people, going to new places, or picking up a book unknown to us, first impressions count for a lot. They can lead to warm, lasting memories or can make us shy away from any future encounters.

Can you recall your own first impressions and earliest memories of reading the classics?

Do you remember wading through pages and pages of text to prepare for an exam? Or were you the child who hid under the blanket to read with a flashlight, joining forces with Robin Hood to save Maid Marian? Do you remember only how long it took you to read a lengthy novel such as *Little Women*? Or did you become best friends with the March sisters?

Even for a gifted young reader, getting through long chapters with dense language can easily become overwhelming and can obscure the richness of the story and its characters. Reading an abridged, newly crafted version of a classic novel can be the gentle introduction a child needs to explore the characters and storyline without the frustration of difficult vocabulary and complex themes.

Reading an abridged version of a classic novel gives the young reader a sense of independence and the satisfaction of finishing a "grown-up" book. And when a child is engaged with and inspired by a classic story, the tone is set for further exploration of the story's themes, characters, history, and details. As a child's reading skills advance, the desire to tackle the original, unabridged version of the story will naturally emerge.

If made accessible to young readers, these stories can become invaluable tools for understanding themselves in the context of their families and social environments. This is why the Classic Starts series includes questions that stimulate discussion regarding the impact and social relevance of the characters and stories today. These questions can foster lively conversations between children and their parents or teachers. When we look at the issues, values, and standards of past times in terms of how we live now, we can appreciate literature's classic tales in a very personal and engaging way.

Share your love of reading the classics with a young child, and introduce an imaginary world real enough to last a lifetime.

Dr. Arthur Pober, Ed.D.

Dr. Arthur Pober has spent more than twenty years in the fields of early childhood and gifted education. He is the former principal of one of the world's oldest laboratory schools for gifted youngsters, Hunter College Elementary School, and former Director of Magnet Schools for the Gifted and Talented for more than 25,000 youngsters in New York City.

Dr. Pober is a recognized authority in the areas of media and child protection and is currently the U.S. representative to the European Institute for the Media and European Advertising Standards Alliance.

Explore these wonderful stories in our
Classic Starts™ library.

Oliver Twist

Pollyanna

The Prince and the Pauper

Rebecca of Sunnybrook Farm

The Red Badge of Courage

Robinson Crusoe

The Secret Garden

The Story of King Arthur and His Knights

The Strange Case of Dr. Jekyll and Mr. Hyde

The Swiss Family Robinson

The Three Musketeers

Treasure Island

The War of the Worlds

White Fang

The Wind in the Willows